Keri

Jan Andrews

A GROUNDWOOD BOOK

DOUGLAS & McINTYRE

VANCOUVER   TORONTO   BUFFALO

Groundwood Books / Douglas & McIntyre
585 Bloor Street West
Toronto, Ontario M6G 1K5

Distributed in the United States by
Publishers Group West
4065 Hollis Street, Emeryville CA 94608

The publisher gratefully acknowledges the assistance of the Canada
Council and the Ontario Arts Council.

Library of Congress data is available

Canadian Cataloguing in Publication Data

Andrews, Jan, 1942-
Keri
ISBN 0-88899-240-8
I. Title.
PS8551.N37K4   1996   jC813'.54   C95-930877-6
PZ7.A53Ke 1996

Design by Michael Solomon
Cover illustration by Harvey Chan
Printed and bound in Canada

To Mim and Kieran
who also keep lights burning

One

"YOUR turn," Mum grunted, with a nod towards the sink.

Rolling her eyes and sighing, Keri got up from the table. It hadn't been much of a lunch now, had it? Not with Mum going on and on all through it. How Keri's teacher had phoned because she hadn't been doing her homework regularly. How Keri had left a plate on the living-room floor. How there weren't enough hours in the day to manage without Keri helping...

Mum nagging the way she'd done ever since last summer, it seemed, when Dad had had to go off working on that ship.

Hanging her head so the strand of wild red hair that always escaped from behind her ear fell forward, Keri gathered the lunch dishes in a pile.

"You're on drying." Mum's nod went to Grae, Keri's brother.

He stood up at once, pushed in his chair and fetched the drying cloth from where it hung over the handle to the oven door.

A fork toppled off the top plate to leave a trail of juice from the baked beans dribbling towards the blue plastic daisies in the vase.

"Don't forget to wipe that up," Mum ordered, as she levered herself to her feet.

From the closed-in porch on the other side of the kitchen door, the sound of the washer churning through a load of wash came at them. Shifting the plates to the counter but ignoring the bean juice, Keri began retrieving the place-mats—the ones Dad had sent with the pictures of St. John's on them, the ones he'd sent when he first left.

"Did you hear me?" Mum asked.

"I always do wipe the table, don't I?" Keri shot back.

Mum's snort said that wasn't quite the truth of it. "I don't know what's got into you. I don't really."

If you don't, you must be crazy, Keri thought.

She watched as Grae took on the task of working the dishcloth over the table's arborite surface. He was rather more thorough than she would have been.

Mum gave her a glare. "Your brother's just turned ten. You're past thirteen. How is it he's the one who's responsible?"

Keri glared right back. As the washer changed its cycle, there was silence for a moment. Through it they heard the grumble of a boat coming in the mouth of Prouty Harbour, plain as anything even though the windows were closed against the late May chill.

Listening and guessing was something they'd done always, so for that moment everything stopped. There was a slight cough, a hesitation in the running of the motor. Keri glanced at her mother. After all, Mum always used to guess. Quick as a wink before Dad even.

There was a look of worry on Mum's face— a frown Keri wasn't expecting.

"Ted James, I reckon," Grae announced. "Been figuring where he'll put his traps in, most like."

He went to the window. Dishes or no dishes, they had to be certain they were right. Keri thought Mum would go upstairs and leave them to it, but she didn't. The boat was Ted's for sure, chugging and labouring through the swell on the water, rising and falling with the lops.

"Why's he coming to our wharf?" Keri demanded.

Mum drew in her breath and bit her lip.

"He asked if he could make use of it. It's nearer his house and he's old now. He's having trouble getting about with that bad leg of his."

Grae stiffened but said nothing.

"It's ours, the wharf," Keri burst out.

"It may be ours but we're not using it, are we?" Mum answered.

"We've got the dory moored there."

"Ted knows that. He's got a dory of his own. He's not going to be needing ours."

"Dad left it specially."

"Yeah, well, we've got to help each other."

"You should have asked us. You shouldn't have just let him."

"He came on me unexpected. I'd just got off work."

"Isn't it bad enough we haven't got our own boat at the wharf any more?"

"For God's sake..."

Letting her words hang in the air, Mum took off for the hallway. From there she could be heard rummaging in the bottom of the hall closet, dragging out the vacuum cleaner and hefting it towards the stairs. Turning back to the window, Keri saw Ted James dock his boat and clamber out with an armful of fish nets.

"He'll be spreading them along the road where Dad always did, drying them in our spot before we know it."

"Of course." Grae spoke at last. "Why not?"

"Why should he?"

"It's the most sensible. We do have to help each other. Mum's only trying to manage."

"Fishing's how we managed."

Keri flung herself towards the sink. She turned the taps on with such a wrench that water sprayed down her front and onto the counter.

"How are we going to feel, with Ted's stuff dumped down everywhere?" she said.

"Maybe it'll be better than having everything all empty."

'You're such a mister nice guy."

"Why not? Why shouldn't we be nice?"

"What about Dad?"

"He doesn't get home much to see. It's been months since his ship came near St. John's. He's so far away, across the ocean."

As Keri got through scrubbing the black guck burnt on the bottom of the bean pan, she heard the long thin moan of the vacuum being switched off. That meant Mum's room was finished. Hers would be next, and she hadn't done even her usual inadequate job of tidying.

"Come on," she said to her brother. "Let's take off."

Grae looked as if he thought they should stay, but the grumble of Ted's motor setting out from the wharf broke in on them. If they stayed, there'd probably be another battle, and battles weren't his thing.

"Where'll we go?" he demanded, as he fed the last of the cutlery into the drawer.

"What's it matter? Let's just get out of here."

They headed for the porch with its jumble of coat hooks, boot trays, tools that hadn't made it to the shed again, the old dresser that was supposed to hold their winter school gear and always had gloves and mittens escaping from its drawers.

Taking down their sweatshirts, they pulled them on.

"Close the door hard," Grae insisted. "You know what Mum said about you leaving it."

"It sticks too much."

"You can do it if you want to."

"You then."

Glad almost of the greyness of the sky and the clouds scudding, Keri leaned into the wind. It tugged at her hair and drove it back behind her. She could see Grae's lifting also, only his was black. Together they plodded down the rough dirt laneway, past the family's beat-up Chevy and onto the road.

The village with its church and houses lay below them. They could see out into the harbour to more wharfs around the shoreline off the rocks. The wharfs were all the same as theirs—pine logs with a small shed, a fishing stage where the gear was kept set towards the middle. There was the government wharf, too, with the long low fish plant halfway along it, where Mum worked.

Usually Keri would scan everything over. She'd check out Gran's old house. She'd even let her gaze go beyond the baseball diamond to that huddle of leftover car parts and shacks where the awful Duffys lived.

Today all she could think about was Ted James.

"Good job Gran isn't here," she muttered. "It'd break her heart."

Actually she was pretty sure her grandmother's heart had been broken when they let the boat go. Gran hadn't said much about it, but Keri still thought the loss had killed her—the shock. She had got old and sick so sudden this past winter. Seemed like one day she was bustling about, making cups of tea and cookies. Next day she wasn't. Then she was in the hospital. All at once—before Dad could get home for it even—Keri and Mum and Grae were filing out of the church behind the coffin, standing with everyone in Prouty, looking in that hole that was her grave.

Ted James wasn't on the wharf any more. He'd left. To get more of his gear, most likely—his lobster traps and the great grey plastic containers to put his catch in. Just the idea of it made Keri want to go down and stand guard. She wanted to get soggy potatoes to pelt him with, to—that was it—to wait till his boat was moored, untie it and set it loose in a storm or something.

But that was unthinkable. Boats were precious. You didn't tamper with them. Even when you were riled as hell and your family didn't have a boat any longer despite the fact that they'd always had one. Even when nothing was fair.

Because it wasn't fair. Dad was a good worker and a good fisherman. It wasn't his fault the ice had come down two years in a row and taken his fish traps out. Who the hell could do anything about icebergs? They were too huge to move. They drifted and swept things away and nothing mattered to them.

It wasn't his fault that replacing the traps with all their nets had cost thousands just when the boat had needed a new engine and that had cost thousands too. It wasn't his fault the catches were so awful.

A scowl set deep on Keri's face. She remembered Dad getting more and more worried, staying out on the water longer and longer, checking his traps. Then coming in one day and telling them the bank manager said he had to sell the boat.

"You can't," Keri had protested.

Mum had just sat there.

"I borrowed and there's no money for the payments," Dad had said.

"How will you fish?"

"That's just it, girl, isn't it? I won't."

"Fishing's our heritage." She'd heard that phrase at school. "We've been a fishing family forever."

For a month nothing had happened except the boat had a FOR SALE sign on it. She'd spent that month figuring out how she could make money. She'd offered her services at Mae Walters' convenience store by the crossroads. She'd reckoned on running away and leaving school. Mailing money back in packets. She'd even saved her allowance, two bucks a week.

Dad had gone to town–to St. John's, a half day's drive away. Apparently the bank manager had suggested it. He'd phoned and said he'd heard there might be something Dad could do.

Late into the evening Keri and Mum and Grae had waited for him in the kitchen. They'd known something was even more wrong when he hadn't been whistling as he got out of the car.

"There's a job," he'd said, as he slumped at the table. "I've taken it but it's away."

Once more, Keri had protested.

"You can't be gone! You can't."

***

"There's nothing else for it. Not now, my girl. They'll put my pay in the bank directly. I'm not sure where I'm going even."

"What's pay got to do with it?"

"Keeps food on the table."

"But we've always had food—our family. Gran's told me. Way back even when Great-grandad was sick, and Gran and her mum had to take the boat out."

"Boat's gone."

Keri had looked to her mother for help.

"You just stop it with your complaining," Mum had said.

"I've a right."

"Not if you can't see, you haven't. Not if you don't know already your dad and I have been over it and over it. Not if you don't know it's hard enough."

The argument she and Mum had begun that evening had gone on and grown more bitter ever since. Even Gran's being sick had been mixed up in it.

"She's getting thinner," Keri had raged. "Why can't you get the doctors to do something? Why can't I go to the hospital to be with her all the time? Why can't I just not bother about school?"

Afterwards had been just as bad. Keri had wanted to keep as much of Gran's stuff as she could, but Mum had said there wasn't room for it. When they'd gone to the house to go through Gran's things—her clothes, her drawers, everything—Mum had insisted they make piles. Keri had tried to sneak more and more onto the pile that was for keeping: Gran's battered old chair, the lamp with the flowers from her bedroom, her jewellery.

"Just what's special," Mum had said, weeding through the pile one more time.

"If she was your mother instead of Dad's..." Keri had countered.

Mum had looked like she might cry. "My mother was dead and buried before I hardly even knew her. Your gran was like a mother to me."

"Well, then."

"You could save every stick she owned all her life. It wouldn't bring her back. That's the truth and you're going to have to know it."

There'd been more, inevitably. Keri would have churned that over in her mind as well, but Grae's voice broke in on her. She realized she'd walked down the road aways, got stuck into staring at their wharf and simply stopped. The hole Grae had dug in the gravel with his toe said how long she'd been there.

"Where'll we go?" he asked again.

All of a sudden she knew that she didn't want to keep on down to the village. Times might be bad, but there was still this buzz of new season excitement in the weeks of waiting for the capelin, the small fish that ran up the beaches to spawn in thousands—the fish that started everything off. Someone would be ready to call out how maybe this year at least the lumpfish would be worth the cost of going out for. How there was some bit of gear that needed fixing.

"If you're going to Alice's, I could see if Josh is home the same time," Grae suggested.

With an effort, Keri forced her eyes round towards the house where Alice lived. Right now though, Alice's wasn't an option.

"Are you kidding?"

Grae's shrug said he gave up.

"There's only one place to go," she ranted.

"Stop being so horrible."

"It's true and you know it. The only place that's ours still is the cove."

Two

THE cove wasn't marked on any map of Newfoundland that Keri had ever come across, but that didn't mean it didn't have a name. It was Rileys' Cove and everyone round Prouty knew it. Gran had been a Riley before she married Grandad, so the cove belonged to them through Gran's family. Had done through hundreds of years, right since some girl had been abandoned there all by herself, in the days when the ships just came and fished for the season, and hardly a soul stayed on the island through the winter anywhere.

Gran had said the girl had almost died. She would have, if a whale hadn't fetched up on the shore when her food was almost gone. The story was so old that Gran hadn't known a lot of details. Still, whenever she'd told it she'd reached up to a shelf and brought down this little padded box. Inside lay a whale bone shaped like a long, curved tooth and wrapped in cotton

---

batting. The bone had a date scratched on it—1762.

The bone was Keri's now. Gran had made a present of it before she'd died. She'd said that's how it had been handed down always, one woman to the next. Keri had set it on her dresser next to the photo of Dad holding the biggest fish he'd ever caught. She'd spread one of Gran's crocheted doilies under it. She'd made a shrine of precious things.

Getting to the cove meant turning back and going up the hill again. There was a certain danger, of course, in passing the house. Once she'd started running, Keri kept her eyes fixed ahead of her, her ears strained against the possibility of Mum calling them for some new chore. She didn't even think to slow down till she was safely beyond the end of the low white picket fence.

That fence was special. Dad had put it up one year when she was younger, when the catch was specially good. They'd had a time almost—a party. Mum, Gran, everyone.

The Donnellys had come from the next house down and then Alice and her folks. Before they knew it, they were in the backyard, the whole lot of them, lighting a fire to sit around.

Theirs was the last house in the village, perched up higher, standing like a marker, its flaking blue paint signalling the openness of all the land around. Beyond it Keri could see the earth stretched—treeless, grass covered, rising and falling—north and west like it went on forever, east to where cliffs dropped sheer towards the shore.

The turnaround for the dead end in the road came quickly. She and Grae crossed it to start out along the track across the neck of the headland and on down. Rileys' was off by itself. It took them almost half an hour to get there. As usual, when they reached the flat grey rock where they could stand and see into the cove, they stopped.

After all, the cove was theirs, and they had Riley names for everything. The Raggeds, round to the right, where at low tide they could scramble out on the rocks the farthest. The Banks, back from the beach, where the patch of dunes rose up. Rileys' Rattle, the stream that appeared out of the earth and, though it ran brown like all the rattles nearby, still flowed water good for drinking. Home Place, where the two small houses that now stood in Prouty (including the one that had been Gran's) had once perched sheltered by the slope.

It was theirs. They'd come here for picnics. They'd fished with rods and lines off the rocks. They'd had cookouts and singsongs.

The houses might be gone, but the wharf was still standing. So was the stage. It had been built by Dad's great-grandfather. You could tell because he'd carved his initials—G.R., George Riley—at the back. Over the years the door had got a bit crooked, but everything else, even the roof, stayed sound.

They always stopped, they always lingered. Always except today.

"What the hell?" Keri yelled as she hurled herself forward.

Her lungs burned and the wind blew hard against her. She just kept pushing onwards, slipping and sliding, until she could fling herself down to where the slope levelled out and the track grew smoother. From there it was two long strides and then she was on the wharf.

A mangled heap of weathered boards covered it. The stage was all destroyed and wrecked. A couple of days ago it had been fine.

"Who'd have done it?" she demanded.

Grabbing up a piece of board, she held it dangling.

"Duffys, most like," Grae gasped, when he'd caught up to her. "Duffys! Has to be."

"What's it to them?"

They both knew though, with the Duffys, it didn't have to be anything more than a stupid drinking spree. Duffys had always been trouble. They were like storms or icebergs. They went on and on, right down to Don Duffy in her class and Mike in Grae's. No doubt there were others to follow.

Duffys! She could see it too, now that she was closer. The scatter of ripped-up parts of the roof along the beach that said what had happened had probably started out with some pathetic game.

"Came round in their boat, like we used to sometimes," Grae guessed.

"They don't deserve a boat."

"If they'd come past the house we'd have heard them, state they must have been in."

Dropping the first piece of wood she'd picked up, Keri pulled out another. She kept on, churning over piece after piece, but the damage was too dreadful. A fragment of the door in one place, a roof stay on top of it.

"So what no one fished out of here any longer. We used it."

"We came in to shelter from the rain. We've left our rods here sometimes and buckets for bait and stuff." Grae squatted to take up a triangle of glass from the window.

"We were going to need it more, now that even our wharf....We could have brought the dory here."

"Dad said he'd never pull it down. Not ever," Grae went on.

Keri wanted to add how it had made her feel safe to come here, but she didn't. Instead she blurted, "Dad said he could remember watching by the cutting tables before he was even old enough to stand. He said it was part of his life."

She lifted up a sliver of door, and an old fishing knife, its blade very thin, its handle worn to nothing, rolled out by her feet. The knife used to lie on a shelf. It wasn't very sharp, but sometimes when Dad had come down with them, he'd picked it up and held it in his hand. "My dad's, this was. Should've buried it with him maybe."

23

"Here." Taking the knife, Keri shoved it in Grae's direction.

"What about you?"

"I dunno." She turned over a few more remnants. "There's nothing else, is there?"

"I don't mind sharing."

They jumped down onto the dark stones of the beach. Splintered off, there was a piece of board with fingermarks rubbed on it. Keri knew where it had come from. It was the place at the corner by the front where everyone had let their hands rest as they'd come round to stow their things away. She'd put her own hand there so often she could have felt the roughness in her sleep.

"You could have that," Grae said.

Grabbing it up, she held it to her. They wandered on through still more mess.

"Makes me want to throw up. Makes me want to string up whoever did it and lynch them."

"There's not even any way we can fix it. Even if we brought Dad when he gets home finally."

Crossing the seaweed at the tide line, they drifted towards the water's edge. Before them the water swelled and heaved. Keri picked up a stone to hurl across it. "We won't have anything left soon. Not anything."

She hurled another stone and then another, not looking at where they fell because she was seeing the inside of her grandmother's house. The kitchen where Gran had sat in the evenings with her feet on the old rag rug Keri had insisted on keeping. It was true the rug was faded—the reds and blues trodden to nothing—but that was only because Gran had made it out of odds and ends of worn-out clothing.

"Dad was born here. This was Gran's home once." Miserably, Grae nodded. Throwing a last stone as hard as she could manage, Keri walked on. "We should have looked after it. First we lose the boat. Then Mum gives away the wharf. Now we let this happen."

"We can't be here every minute."

"We could have set booby traps!"

Even she knew that was ridiculous. The wind tugged harder at her. They weren't halfway to where the beach stones ended and the rocks began when the wreckage seemed to pull at them to turn around.

"Maybe we should just get everything off the

wharf," Grae said. "Otherwise we'll have to climb over it all when the tide's up and we want to put our lines in."

"We can do what we like. The cove won't be the same again."

"It might be better though not having to look at it," Grae persisted.

"What'll we do with the lumber?"

"Pile it up, I guess."

"Have a gigantic bonfire? Invite all the village and burn the Duffys in effigy?" The thought made her grin despite herself. Anyway, Grae was hitching at his jeans the way Dad always did. "If you're so set on it," she said at last.

"You never know. We might be able to build something after."

"A junk heap, most like."

The trouble was, once he'd said it, she couldn't help but imagine.

"It's too late now. I've got to feed my rabbits. If I leave them till after supper, Mum'll only get riled. We can come back tomorrow."

The words "Screw Mum" were on Keri's lips, but all at once she was too tired and fed up to be bothered. There was the fact too that a fine, harsh drizzle was setting in. Still, she had to stalk over and stand by the destruction one more time.

She let her eyes go up the beach to where the old fishing flakes—the racks the catch had been dried on—were set into the ground. The flakes had been placed carefully. Not too long a walk with the fish, but apart and upwind so the fish smell and the flies wouldn't drive folks in the houses blathering mad.

There'd been row upon row of flakes once, Gran had said. Now there were only two still standing. Even those looked like they wouldn't last much longer. The legs were skewed and shaky.

Nevertheless Keri could hear it almost. How Gran had told her it used to be. The two families working together like one big family. Everyone making jokes to keep themselves going because they did get tired. Even the little ones doing something—scraping the fish livers into the oil barrels, sluicing down the cutting tables. Everyone calling back and forth. The boats grinding against the wharf as they came in low and laden.

"The men could hardly get the fish off the

jiggers fast enough. It was that good," Gran had said.

Keri could see it. The cod huge and fat and flapping, being gutted and thrown in heaps, salted and spread on the spruce boughs. Turning to flat stiff boards for shipping as they lay beneath the sun.

The picture was so bright, so vivid. "Don't you wish we could go back again?" she asked.

When she got no answer, she looked behind her, only to realize she was talking to herself. Grae was starting to climb back up the track. A flurry of gulls went over, screaming and mewing to each other. Where the water lapped around the end of the wharf, a wave broke extra high.

As she screwed up her face to watch her brother's small, neat movements, her foot shot out to kick at the pile of boards in anger. Yelling to Grae to wait up and clutching the board with the fingermarks tightly, she set off.

Three

As she dragged herself up the slope, Keri felt the wreck of the stage like an ache between her shoulder blades.

"They never should have moved," she burst out, as she caught up with Grae and stopped for one more look.

"They didn't have any electricity. Nor any water, except what they could carry."

"So what? They kept on fishing." She wrapped her arms around her so the board was close against her chest. "Look at it down there," she demanded. "Look!"

He did for a minute, but then he checked his watch once more. "We've got to hurry."

She toiled along the worn, narrow track behind him, bracing herself for the climb up the steep part where the dark-leaved clumps of bushes grew on either side. At the turnaround in the road, the village lay full in her view again. She stuck her tongue out hard in the direction of Duffys', but it was Gran's house that held her attention. Her eyes bored through the walls to where the old wood bedstead, the little dresser by the door in the hallway, the flowered wallpaper in the living room even, had all been changed so Ron and Trish Walters could move in.

"They never should have let them bring the houses from the cove," she persisted.

"The government said they had to. Come on."

"You're such a nag!"

"We'd never get home if I wasn't."

He left her to tromp up the laneway and went off to his rabbit pen behind the shed. The windows at the washer end of the porch were steamed up, but not so badly that Keri couldn't see Mum's outline, all tall and stark, inside. Opening the door with a hefty sideswipe from her bum, she found herself surrounded by soggy heaps of laundry. The dryer had quit again.

"You cut it fine enough," Mum said. She was putting in a load of jeans. "Where were you anyway?"

"Down at Rileys'."

"Rileys'! That's all you think about."

"The stage is wrecked."

"It doesn't strike you as odd you'd take off on me without doing a hand's turn, any more than you had to?"

"Duffys have ruined it."

"Back you come now, waltzing in at the last minute."

"They've smashed it in pieces."

"It's only an old shed."

"Our great-great-grandfather built it."

"He may have, but what I care about right now is you getting in to set the table."

Mum poured in the detergent and slammed down the lid of the washer. The clamour of the machine made throwing back the retort in Keri's throat too difficult. Kicking her sneakers into the boot tray, she clumped through the kitchen door.

"Get that sweatshirt off. It's damp," Mum called after her.

Keri took no notice. For a moment she thought about taking the board up to her room, but when her eyes fell on the vase, she propped it there instead. It hid the plastic daisies, but so what? Mum had some idea they cheered things up. She'd come home with them from the supermarket just after Christmas. Take more than a few flowers, Keri had reckoned even then.

"What did you do? Mum's riled as anything," Grae whispered after he got in.

"I told her about the stage. She wouldn't listen."

"It's Saturday..."

"What difference does it make what day it is?"

"You know Saturday and Sunday evenings are home time. We're supposed to be together."

"If she'd pay some attention..."

They got no further because Mum appeared with a basket of clothes from before the dryer had quit for Grae to take upstairs.

"What's that doing there?" she demanded, seeing the board. "It's got no business...not when I've been cleaning." She snatched it off the table and planked it on the window ledge. "Bits of wood belong in the shed if they belong anywhere."

"It's not just any old bit of wood. It's from the cove."

"Find another home for it."

"It's the one everyone touched. It ought to be in a...a museum."

"Are you gone in the head or something?" Already Mum was reaching for the jar of utensils by the sink and taking out the potato masher. "If you think those were the glory days, you should have been there to try it." She started in on the potatoes. "We're not the only ones to lose things, you know. There have been lots of others before us. There'll be more too before we're finished. You should hear what they're saying." She was mashing the potatoes harder and harder.

"New season's not what I want to hear about."

"New season? You're not listening! What makes you think this year's going to be any better? There aren't the fish any more. That's all there is to it. Your dad's just one of many. There'll be more boats sold this year most like than you can imagine. And there's not everyone that'll be able to get jobs...here, there, anywhere! We should think ourselves lucky."

From outside, above the gathering sound of the wind, came the cough of Ted James' motor. Mum paused.

Letting her hair fall forward so she could hide behind it, Keri set out salt, pepper and ketchup in three great thunks.

Mum drew in her breath. "Look, I'm sorry. You're right. I should have asked you. And maybe I shouldn't have let him. I'm sorry about the stage too. I know it means a lot to you."

Keri sank into silence. Grae's glance went from one to the other of them as he slipped back through the doorway.

"We've got to get on with it," Mum said. "We've got to do the best we can."

Still Keri said nothing.

"Let's just have a supper with no quarrelling. You like sausages and mashed potatoes, and there's a good roast for tomorrow."

Having set out the cutlery with as much shift and clatter as she could manage, Keri shovelled the food down without tasting it. She swallowed the fresh-from-the-freezer storebought cake that was Saturday's treat without uttering a word.

All the while she was thinking that if Dad had been there, he'd have been riled as hell. He'd have joined them in railing against

Duffys. They'd have had a good rant together. He'd have hot-footed it back to the cove without thinking about eating, probably. He'd at least have asked them if there was anything they planned to do.

The tension was too much for Grae. He kept opening his mouth and closing it, getting paler by the minute. The washer rumbling away in the background filled the space between them.

"You could at least give me a bit of talk," Mom protested, as soon as it let up.

They were drinking their after-supper tea by that time. Keri curled her lip while Grae searched for some safe subject.

"I got this book from the library. It's about shipwrecks. There's a map of the Grand Banks and everything."

"Shipwrecks? Couldn't you have found something more cheerful?"

"What else would he get? Our life's a wreck, isn't it?" The words were out of Keri's mouth before she'd thought them.

"What's that you said?" Mum snapped.

Gathering herself together, Keri stared her mother in the face.

"Our life's a wreck," she repeated.

———

Mum got to her feet. "You never let up, do you?"

"It's not why I was telling you..." Grae faltered.

"No, I don't expect it was," Mum said. "You've got a bit more sense. You though—you, my girl—there's no end to you, is there? You never give anyone a chance."

Keri pushed her chair back. In the process, she knocked over her water. Mum's eyes blazed. She looked like she was going to explode, like she was going to yell louder than she'd yelled ever. Instead her jaw tightened and she cleared the plates.

"Mum," Grae pleaded, but she took no notice.

Using the dish cloth, she wiped the table over end to end. When it was clean, she went out through the kitchen door and up the stairs. Keri heard the sound of drawers and closets opening and closing above them.

By the time Mum came back, she'd taken off the jeans and rough checked shirt she used for housework and changed into a blouse and dress pants. She had her old black purse under her arm.

"I'm going down to Jenks'."

"Mum, please," Grae said.

"They asked me and I told them no, it's our time together. Why I bothered, I can't think." Heading out to the porch, she fetched her jacket. "I want you in bed when I get back," she ordered as she forced her arms into the sleeves. "I want you in bed, the pair of you. And I want this kitchen cleared. You understand? And you remember. Sunday's the day I take my lie in. The week's hard enough."

"You don't have to bother yourself. We've got work to do. We've got the cove to get to. We're going to clear the mess up. We won't go waking you!" Keri shot back.

"Well, if you're going, you go quiet. But remember. I've got that roast. You be back early."

The slamming of the outside door made the house shake. Mum was gone.

Four

KERI was out of the kitchen and pounding up the stairs in an instant.

"Bitch," she spat out, as she stood at her bedroom window.

She watched while Mum hurried down to the village, her body bent forward because now the drizzle had turned to rain, and she was forcing herself against it into the wind.

A gust blew stronger, catching at her mother's wiry brown hair. Hair was the only feature Keri hadn't got from her.

"Like sisters the two of you. Going to be the same height, most like. Those long legs of yours." How often had she heard that one?

"Keri," Grae called up to her. She pretended she hadn't heard.

Mum rounded the corner at the bottom of the hill and swung right into Jenks' driveway. Without a look behind her, she disappeared from sight.

"Keri." There was the sound of water going in the sink now.

If Grae wanted to be a wimp and do the dishes for both of them, he could. She wasn't budging. Not that her room felt like it was where she wanted to be yet. There was too much evidence of her mother's tidying. Keri had to rattle about getting the closet open so the poster of the punk rocker with green spiked hair was visible. She had to shift the dragon on the window ledge back to its proper place beside the shell garden Alice had given her for her birthday; to rumple the checkered green bedspread so it looked like somewhere she might sit.

Only then could she take the peanut butter jar off the top of her dresser where she kept it next to her precious-things shrine. The jar held the money she'd gone on saving to bring Dad back.

Each time she counted it, she hoped it somehow might have doubled. Even though it hadn't, touching the money reminded her that she was at least trying. She put the bills and coins back safely and reached for the whale bone in its box.

She removed the lid and undid the cotton

batting so she could stroke the numbers of the date and whisper them over, "One, seven, six, two." She lifted out the bone and sat down on Gran's old rug. Holding the smooth white shape so tightly that the sharp pieces dug into her palm, she started to make pictures of the girl.

Gran hadn't known what the girl looked like, but Keri could imagine. The girl had come from Ireland most like. Keri was almost certain she was the source of her own red hair. After all, Gran had had red hair too when she was young, and the girl was her ancestor.

Keri always saw the girl wearing a long skirt, because that's what women had worn in those days. The skirt was rough and thick and grey. Only rich people had bright colours, and the girl was poor. Still she wore a band of blue-green fabric over one shoulder. Keri had seen a band like that once in a book. The band was mostly for decoration. It wasn't enough to keep her warm. For that she had to have a shawl. Several, in fact, to wrap around her against the winter's cold.

The girl was standing on the beach with the ships sailing away from her. She wasn't crying or feeling sorry for herself. She was shaking her fist and screaming curses, so even the sailors were afraid. She was following the ships around the clifftop to yell down on the men again, standing with her hands on her hips and her feet spread in a way that said the cove was hers and she was glad of it.

From there Keri got on to how she'd lived. The other tilts—the shacks—on the beach were all empty and dirty. Hers had bits of fabric for curtains over the window and jars of grasses she'd gathered for decoration. There was a broken piece of mirror so she could see herself and keep herself neat. She would comb her hair back with her fingers and tie it with a ribbon, washing out of a canvas bucket with water she'd brought from the rattle, rinsing her clothes and spreading them to dry on the rocks.

Keri was just beginning to wonder if she should make a picture of the girl learning to snare rabbits when she heard Grae climbing the stairs. Before he got to the top, she slipped the bone into her pocket.

"There's a special on TV about Antarctica," he told her from the doorway.

She hadn't exactly planned to spend the

evening on snow and penguins, but he was hitching at his jeans again, and he'd got a look on his face that she had a weakness for—his head on one side, his eyes all hopeful.

"You going to watch?" she asked.

His face lit up and he nodded. Downstairs in the living room, she scrunched up in the corner of the couch and pulled the orange and purple afghan Mum had won in the raffle at the church bazaar over her. She let her hand go to her pocket so she could keep on making the pictures in her head.

The special proved to be a good backdrop. It made her think how brave the girl had been. It made her listen to the wind outside and see the cove.

"Where did you put the knife?" she asked, when the commercials came on.

"In my drawer. I wanted to show it to Mum, but you two were fighting."

"She wouldn't even have looked at it most likely."

The commercials ended. A description of how Antarctic seals have whiskers on their chins to keep their ice holes open followed. In the kitchen, the phone rang. At first Keri flung off the afghan to get up because she thought it might be Alice. Then their quarrel came back to her.

"You're so crabby always," Alice had said.

"How else do you expect me to be?"

"I don't know, but I'm tired of it."

Keri had stomped off. A week had gone by. Alice hadn't spoken to her since. And if Alice didn't phone her, sure as hell no one else would.

She left the answering to Grae.

"We think it was Duffys," she heard him saying.

"You don't have to tell the whole world," she yelled through the open door.

The special came to an end. Flicking channels, they found a movie about outer space. Grae didn't like it much. First he went and made them both hot chocolate. Then he announced that he was going to bed.

"If we're going to Rileys', we'll have to get up early," Keri declared.

"Maybe we shouldn't go tomorrow. Maybe we should wait a while."

"Duffys won't come back. Not in the daytime. You don't have to fuss yourself."

———

"It's Mum. I think she's lonely."

"Some way she's got of showing it."

"She misses Dad."

"She didn't do anything to stop him going."

"She couldn't. She's worried. You heard what she said about the fishing. The plant'll go in the end."

"She grumbles enough about it. 'Up to my elbows all day in snow crab!'"

He tried another tack. "We'll have to be awful quiet not to wake her."

"We've had enough practice other Sundays."

His nod said he'd given in. If he hadn't, Keri would have told him they'd stay home tomorrow over her dead body. After all, cleaning up the stage had been his idea in the first place, and by now the wind was blowing so strong it was rattling the windows. The pieces of roof would be going every which way. The two of them would have to get on with it if they wanted even the chance of building something else.

"I'll set my alarm. I'll come and get you," she said. "We'll get up at eight like we used to do when we went out with Dad."

As soon as she heard his bed creak, she took the bone out to look at. Then it occurred to her that if she didn't go to bed herself soon, she'd land up facing Mum. She went into the kitchen to prop the board back in front of the vase. Upstairs, she slipped the bone beneath her pillow so she could lie with it under her head.

For a while she occupied herself with figuring how to find a way to write to Dad. Maybe if he knew about the stage, he'd decide he couldn't stay away any longer.

The slap of the lops on the shore seemed louder. There was a dog barking—Dawn Donnellys', most like.

More minutes ticked by. Footsteps sounded on the gravel. The door to the porch was forced open and then closed. Keri didn't think her mother would have seen her light, but she wasn't taking any chances, so when she heard Mum coming up the stairs, she made her breathing extra deep.

Still, when the light appeared under her doorway, she was filled with a sudden longing to call out. To have her mother come and sit on the end of the bed and talk to her. To tell her one of John Jenks' famous boring jokes.

Mum did stop, too. She waited outside, listening. Another chewing out was all Keri would let herself think. Bringing the image of the girl yelling at the sailors into her mind, she held herself motionless.

At last her mother moved on.

From the bathroom Keri heard water running and the toilet being flushed. Mum went past Keri's door on her way to her own room.

Finally there was that squeak and sighing from her bed that was like no other. Keri put her hand under her pillow so that she could feel the bone's shape one more time before she slept.

Five

TWICE Keri woke in the night. The first time she'd been dreaming. The girl was in the dream. She was holding a baby, and the baby was a girl as well. Keri didn't know how she knew that. She just did.

The baby was laughing because the girl was holding her up to watch the way the clouds were flying. When the baby laughed, the girl laughed, clasping her daughter close to her, proud as proud.

For a while Keri lay in the darkness reliving the dream, thinking how Gran had said the girl might easily have had a baby. A baby might have been the reason she'd been left behind. She tried to remember if the baby in the dream had had red hair.

That time the wind was still blow-moaning round the tool shed. The next time Keri woke, the wind had died. The world outside was filled with the *whu-up, whu-up* of the fog warning from the light on Prouty Point.

The fog still hung heavy in the morning. She saw it swirling grey and moist through the gap between the drapes as she opened her eyes at the pinging of the alarm. Quick as she could, she reached for the alarm's button.

Mum's bed let out its squeak, but there was no other sign of movement. It flicked through Keri's mind how when she and Grae had gone out with Dad on Sundays, he had always taken Mum tea in bed. He'd set it on a tray with a jug for the milk and the teapot they'd got from their wedding that was kept for special occasions.

Careful about being quiet, Keri slid her feet to the floor. While she was picking up her clothes from where she'd dropped them, the dream came back to her. She reached under her pillow, took out the bone, squeezed it and put it in her pocket.

Grae was awake already, sitting up in his pyjamas reading his shipwreck book.

"Bring the knife," she whispered.

Downstairs, she grinned in satisfaction at the sight of the board still on the table. She was annoyed though that her mother had planked her purse down right nearby, with a note propped against it: HOPE YOUR WORK GOES WELL. Keri scrunched up the note and threw it in the garbage. She moved the purse to the counter so the board could stand alone.

"I'm going to make lunch," she decided, as they ploughed through cereal and toast with peanut butter and molasses.

"We're not going to stay out all day, are we?" Grae asked, watching her pile the bologna sandwiches high.

"We might if we need to."

Finding pleasure in finishing the loaf, she counted out six apples and made hot chocolate. She put the hot chocolate in the two big thermoses Dad used to take out on the boat with him instead of in the stupid little ones Mum had got for her and Grae for school.

"Get your backpack," she ordered, when she was nearly done.

"There's all the washing out in the porch still," Grae reported.

"So?"

"I just thought..."

"Not much good us hanging it out in the fog, now is it?"

"You don't think we should just go up and say goodbye to her?"

"You know what she told us about waking her. You're crazy."

"All day's long. With Dad we only ever went out for the morning."

Keri rolled her eyes. She shoved the last of the sandwiches in the bread bag and zipped the backpack. "All she said was we had to be back in time for the damn roast."

"At least we should put the dishes in the sink."

Leaving him to it, she went to get her jacket. When he joined her, he reached into the pouch of his sweatshirt, took out the knife and transferred it to the front pocket of the backpack.

He still had to see to his rabbits, of course. Normally she liked to watch how they let him stroke them, how they went into a trance almost when he rubbed the place behind their ears. Today she was too eager to get going.

"I'll wait by the car," she said.

The fog was folding around itself so thick that she could hardly see the end of the laneway. Duffys', Jenks', Ted James', Alice's, even Donnellys' were blotted out. It seemed the best that could happen.

There was no one else around anyway, as far as she could tell. Sundays were for quiet, even in the season. That's what had made it extra good that Dad had taken them out then.

They hadn't fished, of course. They had gone in the boat just cruising, taking turns at the wheel, steering through the tickles—the narrows between islands—stopping in inlets that weren't on the trap-checking route.

She was remembering with bitterness how it had felt to stand beside him with the throb of the engine coming up through her feet and legs, how good she was at holding the boat steady, when Grae came scurrying up.

He glanced towards Mum's window. "I don't like it, having that fight and not even seeing her."

Keri responded with a mammoth shrug.

There might be fog, but they could have found their way to the cove with their eyes closed. Beside the track, the grass was covered with soft bright fog drops. Grae had worn boots, but Keri had stuck with her sneakers.

Sounds were muffled, so mainly they walked across the headland in silence.

———

The farther they got, the more Keri became aware of the bone in her pocket scratching through the fabric of her jeans. She could have moved it, but she didn't. The more it scratched, the more it seemed like the pack on her back was weighted not just with lunch but with supplies, the more she could get into pretending she was the girl.

She began walking with longer strides, the way she figured the girl must have. She settled the pack on her shoulders so it sat just right. She imagined what the girl's skirt would have felt like around her legs. She touched her shoulder as if she might find the band of blue-green fabric there.

On foggy days like this, the girl would have stayed in her tilt as much as she could, most likely. Not that the fog would have bothered her but, if there had been a baby, she would have had to look after it. She would have told her daughter stories, taken her hands to play that Hot Pies game that Gran knew. She would have waited for the child to fall asleep so she wouldn't be frightened when she went out to get water or wood for the fire.

The lookout rock loomed before them. A

wheezing *ha-ar* came drifting from below. For a moment Keri thought she'd imagined that too. Then she realized Grae had stopped short to listen.

"Can't be," he was muttering.

"Can if you can hear it."

"But it's too early. Whales don't get here till after the capelin."

Hurrying now, she pushed on towards the steep part. From there the sound was unmistakeable. When her hand went to her pocket, the bone seemed to leap into her fingers.

"That's a whale blow and you know it," she called out.

Six

THE track grew narrower. There were twists and zigzags. Still Keri kept going as quickly as she could. If there were whales, she wanted to see them—rolling and lolling on the water, blowing and heaving themselves over, diving and coming to the surface to blow again. Gran had said there hadn't been whales in the cove since that first one, as far back as anyone could remember. Besides, if she could see whales now, it would be a bit like a real Sunday out with Dad.

He might complain about whales—how they got caught in the nets, how they weren't good for anything except attracting tourists. Somehow though when there were whales around, he'd always slow the boat and watch.

"Our family's got to be grateful to them," he'd said once. "Without whales, maybe we wouldn't be here."

The murmur of the rattle came at them

more distinctly, telling her they'd gone past the flakes. The *pu-ssh* and *pu-sshing* of the lops rose clearer. They reached Home Place. The pile of lumber was becoming visible.

"Right off the end of the wharf," Keri cried, as the long *ha-ar* broke on the air again.

"Over to the right aways," Grae objected.

"We'll go on the beach then."

Keeping her eyes fixed on the water, she started out across the clatter of the stones.

At first she thought she was seeing some great rock, but it was a rock where no rock should be. It had a snout all blunt and V-shaped. The snout started just below the tide-line and became a body. It flowed on into the water. Somewhere there must be tail flukes.

"Holy," she murmured and stood stock still.

Letting the pack slide off her shoulders, she walked forward to where she could feel the seaweed and the smaller stones under her feet.

"Ker!" Grae's cry came at her as a warning.

The whale's jaw was grounded on the seabed. Its mouth curved down and under. There were long deep ridges flowing beneath its chin. It had barnacles and great huge bumps with whiskers sticking from them.

"We've never been so close. Not ever," she called out.

"We'll have to be careful or we'll frighten it."

Figuring she would go as far along the whale's side as she could, Keri bent to roll up her jeans. The great shape stayed unmoving.

Her right hand went back to her pocket. It occurred to her that the girl would have come bursting out of her tilt clutching her shawl around her, just like they'd come bursting through the fog. The day might even have been foggy. The girl would have thought the whale was a rock like they had. She'd have stopped to gasp in wonder. She wouldn't have been able to help herself, not with it lying there, so long and big. Long as the school bus, Keri reckoned. Long as the ship the girl had come in maybe.

The chill of the water bit into Keri's ankles. She saw the whale's eye—an enormous ball set deep in its head—following her progress from under the water, moving as she moved.

"It knows we're here," she cried.

The whale blew again, so loud and so sudden that she was caught unawares. Steam shot high from behind the head, and spray fell over her.

"The blow's different because it's on the land," Grae said.

She didn't answer because she was too busy imagining the girl getting wet and shaking the drops out of *her* hair as well.

The fog thinned and collected itself and rolled in thicker. The fin high on the whale's back appeared for a moment, got swallowed up in the mist and disappeared once more.

"There was one before and now there's another," Keri whispered.

She pictured the girl's relief, felt the happiness that must have come surging through her, how she must have wanted to dance.

The water was halfway up Keri's calves. As she turned to wade back, she went faster. "Come on. Come and look properly," she yelled.

Trusting that Grae wouldn't be able to hold out much longer, she started off along the whale's other side. Aware that here too an eye was watching her, she peered through the fog to where the fins stretched sideways. The edges facing her were white. Keeping her right hand in her pocket, she reached out with her left to touch the whale's skin. The whale didn't respond in any way, so she began stroking it. Finally Grae got to her.

"Doesn't it mind?"

"I don't think so. Feel it. It's all warm."

"Of course. It's the same temperature we are. The exact same almost."

"Its skin's all smooth and silky."

Grae's face softened the way it did when he was with his rabbits. As he reached out too, he started crooning. "It's all right then. We won't hurt you."

The whale blew one more time. If it hadn't been for their jackets, they'd have been soaked.

As they waded round its snout once more, Keri found herself taking a little hop-skip step, because the weight of the awfulness of her life was dropping from her. It might not last, but just for this day she could almost laugh at the thought of Mum getting out of bed and raging around about how she was thoughtless and irresponsible. Keri could look towards the headland and pretend she didn't have to go back to Prouty ever.

"It's a miracle, this is," she burst out.

"How can you say that? It won't be able to get off again. It's going to have to die here."

"When the time comes, it'll use its fins."

"The fins are for balance. It can't move them. I read about it in a book."

Keri drew back the hand that had been stroking the whale, but even as she did so she felt the curve of the bone against her other palm. A picture came to her of the girl making a place for her baby to sleep out of feathers she'd collected.

The answer seemed simple.

"There's not so much of it on the bottom."

"What's that got to do with it?"

"It's only like a boat." Grae's frown kept deepening. "It only wants the tide. With the tide we can launch it." Her brother shuffled from foot to foot, biting his lip as if there was something he wanted to say. "We've pushed enough boats off." Her glance went towards Home Place. "They floated the houses."

"It's not a house."

"Of course not. It's alive. It'll swim as soon as it can help itself. The water line's higher every minute. High tide can't be more than half an hour."

"More like three quarters." The spout of the whale's breath soared over them, and a wave

59

washed near Grae's boot-tops. He hitched at his jeans in discomfort.

"Three quarters of an hour's nothing."

He didn't argue but, for a long moment, he stared towards the headland, biting his lip and screwing up his face.

Keri's sneakers were sodden. She waded back beyond the tide line and thawed out her feet so she would be ready when the time came to push the whale off. Jumping up and down and wiggling her toes, she gazed through the fog into the distance where the whale would go.

Gran would have been pleased to hear about this, she reckoned. Gran would have taken off her apron and sat Keri down and made her tell the story at least three times.

Grae came to join her, but he still seemed uneasy.

"Got muddled up in the fog. That's how it got here, I reckon."

Keri was barely listening. She was seeing the girl in triumph in the spring. The ships were sailing in and the sailors and the fishermen were crowding round her. They were congratulating her, saying she'd held the cove for them so no one else could get it. They were treating her like a heroine, but she was holding her head so they had to look straight at her. She was letting them know she hadn't forgotten what they'd done.

"I think it's a humpback," Grae added.

"A whale is a whale is a whale, Dad says," Keri shot back.

Grae grinned and set out to wade along the whale's side again. He cupped his hands to pick up some water. Letting go of it slowly, he dribbled it above the whale's mouth. The whale's skin moved in a ripple of what seemed like pleasure.

Grae's eyes lit up.

"You like that, don't you?" he murmured.

When Keri tried it, the same thing happened. They both reached into the water again and again. The whale was so big though.

"We'd do better with bailers," she joked.

"There's bleach bottles from floats all over. I've got the knife too so we could cut the bottoms off."

They went to pick up a couple of plastic bottles from under the wharf. The knife didn't cut too well—more like hacking with the edges coming rough.

"After this, I'll sharpen it and I'll keep it sharp," Grae promised.

A stearin started hovering along the beach, its forked tail flashing. Worrying that the bird might attack the whale, Keri prepared to run, waving her arms. The stearin dived, came up with a small silver fish in its beak and moved on. The fog warning was still *whu-up, whu-up*ing from Prouty.

"There's only a square of the jaw that's stuck now," Keri announced.

That square was getting freer by the minute. The tide had got to where all of a sudden the water seemed to be rushing to eat the space up faster. The whale's mouth was immersed completely. Only the top of its back was uncovered.

"If it was a boat, we'd have to get started," Keri declared.

"By the fins would be best, but it's awful deep there."

As she thought of Dad, standing in his waders by the dory, she was tempted to tell her brother they had to try it. But the fins were as thick as boat sides, and he would be almost out of his depth. She didn't want him drowning.

She looked at the fins and back again.

"The head's the bit we've got to get off first."

A wave rolled past her to lap at the high-water mark. It turned and churned at the seaweed, so she could hear the stones being flung up and set down again. While the wave lasted, the whale's jaw rose off the seabed. Its body was held uplifted.

"This is it then," Keri yelled.

The wave sucked back round her legs so the whale sank and grounded. All they had to do was wait for another one that was bigger. Keri gave the bone a squeeze.

"Every seventh, is it?" she demanded.

Grae was beside her, his hands set, his face flushed with expectation. She started counting before he could even nod.

"Almost seven!"

The whale floated a little longer. A little and a little with each wave swelling and lifting till not one bit of the whale's body was on the bottom. From where the fog and water met, the curling crest of a roller was heading in towards them.

"Come on," she cried. "So it can catch the back race. Come on. Get ready. Push." They did but it was too late. "Next time we'll have to start sooner."

The water they were standing in grew deeper. There was so much of the whale submerged that whether the waves were coming in or going back its body was floating, falling and rising free.

"Push. Push hard."

"It's not moving."

"It will in a minute. Push!" She had barnacles under her hands. They dug in and hurt, but the girl must have hurt often, toiling away all by herself. Just staying alive must have been some effort. "Get your back into it."

"I am."

"Bend your knees then. Think about it all plunging and lunging through the water."

The waves began chopping and dancing out of rhythm. They swelled higher, breaking on the beach with more noise and shushing. Stones were being thrown against Keri's ankles. There was the sound of slapping on the surface.

"Its tail must be moving. I told you it would start swimming," she called out.

The waves pouring in through the mist were

longer, stronger. The water was frothing. There was foam all over.

She had to grab Grae, because he was being thrown off balance. A few more seconds and he'd have lost his footing completely.

As Keri stumbled over the tideline, she knew one thing was certain. The whale had been pushing against them. The whale was driving itself forward up onto the beach.

Seven

T HE whale was fighting so hard to get on
land that in the end all Keri could do was
watch it. She couldn't even think of wading
back into the water until the breakers had qui-
eted and its jaw was held firm on the bottom
once again.

"We did something wrong," she muttered.

"It's what I knew from the beginning." Grae
was kicking the stones about in anguish. "I
should have said sooner."

"Said what?"

"I just kept hoping. Whales don't get lost in
the fog. They have radar. They travel across
oceans. They can navigate better than boats
even." He paused and sighed. "It's the way it
always happens when they're beached."

"It wasn't beached. It was just—"

"There was one up by Trinity, remember? It
was on TV and in the papers."

She did remember vaguely. Everyone had

been talking about it. How mostly the people who were racing to the rescue were mainlanders. How they were always interfering.

"Care more about whales than they do about us," the talk in the village had been. But that was when Gran had gone to the hospital, and Keri had been missing her, hating how she couldn't go to her grandmother's house after school. She'd been scheming how when Gran came home she'd go down to live with her because she'd need looking after.

"What's Trinity got to do with it?"

"It's an example. They towed the one there out to sea even."

"I bet if we had gone by the fins..."

"It wouldn't have mattered. It's hurt. It's wounded."

"You can't see anything."

"That was in the book as well. They can be hurt inside where no one can see..." The crack in his voice got the better of him for a moment. "It's all mixed up with how they're mammals. When they're hurt, they get this idea they can breathe on land easier and rest up a bit."

"So?"

"I'm trying to explain what's happening. I'm

trying to tell you there's something wrong with it, but it thinks here on land it can heal itself."

The whale let out its breath. "It's still breathing, isn't it?" Her mind raced. "If it's still breathing and it's still alive, it could just want looking after. If it's trying to heal itself, we could help it."

There was a pause before Grae answered. "We don't know what to do."

"I bet it said in that book of yours. I bet if you think..."

"It just said to be kept alive...cetaceans have to be kept wet. That's how they're moved to aquariums and places."

"So we were doing the right thing without even knowing it. We just have to keep going."

"The book said it's a theory. I don't think anyone has ever proved it."

"There's always a first time."

Before she knew it, she was bringing the bone out to show him. She was telling him how last night, for the first time ever, she hadn't left it in its box.

"I dreamed about the girl," she went on. "I think...I think it's like the girl called the whale here because she knew we'd help it."

His eyes told her how much he wanted to believe the whale's life could be saved. Nonetheless, he squatted to pick up a handful of beach stones and let them run through his fingers before he answered. "It wouldn't hurt to try, I guess."

"We'll get our bailers again. We dropped them but we can get them easy. They're only floating out a bit."

He looked once more towards the headland.

"You don't think we should tell Mum, do you?"

"Why?"

"Because we always used to whenever anything important happened."

"She'll still be in bed."

"At this hour?"

"The mood she's in, if we tell her, she'll stop us. You'll be wanting to tell the whole village next."

"No, I won't."

"It's our secret. We can't tell anyone."

"Mum's not anyone." The edges of his mouth went tight.

Grabbing apples from the pack—one for herself and one to shove in his direction—Keri fixed her eyes on the whale's huge body. She trudged off, furious, her mind set on the work ahead.

A bailerful of water left a patch of the whale's skin all dark and wet and gleaming, but the patch was pretty small, and there was always so much left untouched. They were going to have to carry and carry. Not that she minded, of course. It must have been like this in the old days. They had walked a million miles a day in the season, so Gran had said.

The whale was so big that right from the beginning she and Grae took different sides. Its bulk loomed between them so they hardly even saw each other except when they had to switch from one side to the other. The switching was Grae's idea.

"You're taller," he said. "You can get the water up higher."

They found extra bailers so they had one for each hand. As Keri tilted the water over the whale's head, the ripple came often.

"We'll have you fixed up in no time," she told it.

Wherever she went, the eye on that side followed her. Once when she set her foot too close by accident, the whale got nervous. Its eyelid shut so fast it was like the slamming of a door. After that she was more careful.

"I think it's a female," Grae said one time when they were passing each other.

"How do you know?"

"Females are smaller."

She wondered if it might have a baby some-where. The idea made her think about the girl. She pictured her bringing her daughter down to the water's edge, stroking her hair and telling her how everything would be all right.

The morning wore on. It became clear that they couldn't keep trudging on forever. They had to have breaks. At first Keri was worried they weren't being tough enough. Then she remembered Gran telling her how the men had rested by leaning against the stage, standing in the sun and smoking. From that, she figured out a system—fifteen minutes of carrying with five off to uncurl their backs and shake out their arms.

"You've got the watch," she said to Grae.

They weren't only getting tired though. They were getting cold and wet. The whale kept blowing as regular as clockwork. The spray fell over them so their hair was plastered against their heads. The water was icy. By the time they got to their breaks, their fingers and toes were numb. The breaks weren't long enough to get the circulation going.

All of a sudden, Keri remembered that she had matches in her jacket pocket. She'd grabbed them up from Gran's when they were going through her door for the last time. They'd been in her jacket so long, she had forgotten about them.

Taking them out, she looked at the pieces of roof from the stage still scattered all around. She figured it would be right to use those if they had no choice. It's what people in the old days would have done. For now there was driftwood in The Banks though. Tromping off with Grae to gather it in armfuls, she set to, lighting a fire.

At first, because of the fog and damp, she couldn't get the fire going. Small tongues of flame leaped and licked for a few moments, only to fade to smoke. She had to dig out all her old gum wrappers and use some scribblings Grae had in his backpack for a project on the weather. She had to send him to The Banks for extra twigs for kindling before she could be sure the blaze would last. Still, she managed.

"If we put more wood on when we take our breaks, we should be able to keep it going," she announced.

By that time, most of the whale's head had inched clear of the water. She remembered how Grae had said it was a humpback. She'd heard about humpbacks being the ones that made those singing noises.

Maybe it'll sing for us, she thought.

When Grae said he was thirsty she sent him to get a drink from the rattle so they could keep the hot chocolate for when they really needed it. She counted the sandwiches, reckoning they should hold off eating any until lunch time and then ration themselves half each per hour so they could keep up their strength.

"We'll have to go round the fins before we're done," Grae told her, checking the water line.

She grinned. Sometimes she'd take a moment to look at the fire through the fog and think how she'd got everything organized. She'd hold the bone and feel the girl was there.

Noon came, with Grae announcing it to the minute, the way he'd announced all the breaks.

She decided they could sit by the fire a while longer. Longer breaks at lunch time must have been another tradition.

The air stayed still and fogbound. With all the hours that had gone by, Keri decided to check the whale over to see if there was any evidence that it was getting better.

She was certain the fact that there was no blood anywhere was a good sign. If it had been bleeding, she'd have seen the blood on the water.

Dreams came of how maybe when the whale was saved they could tell people. Their names would be in the papers and they'd be famous—rich even. They'd buy another boat. Dad would come home. He'd be a fisherman again.

One dream led to another. She was well into picturing a new stage, maybe even houses, when she noticed that the ends of her hair were ruffling a little in the breeze.

Eight

"WIND'S coming up," Grae said.
For some reason he seemed worried.
Keri took no notice. She watched in delight as
the fog stirred and lifted so that soon the mist
around her was beginning to drift and dance in
wisps. All this while the fog-warning had been
sounding in the distance. At last it stopped. As
blue sky started to appear, Keri flung off her
jacket.

For the girl, the warm days must have been
wonderful. The girl would have been able to
bring her baby out while she aired the tilt.
She'd have loosened the bundlings all around
her daughter, carried her up to the clifftop,
shown her birds and plants.

The cove was clear now, right to the
entrance. There were sun-sparkles glistening on
the water. Keri pulled off her sweatshirt and
jeans. It was years since she and Grae had been
in their underwear together, but she didn't care.

"If we spread our jeans out now, they'll be dry later," she declared, as Grae stripped to his T-shirt and underwear as well.

It was only an hour—an hour and a quarter at most—to the tide's turning. From then on everything would be easier. The water would begin to rise, and the whale would feel it coming. Maybe it would even call out to its companions. Maybe they'd come to the cove to join it.

The bone was tucked down safely in her jeans pocket. The next time they were by the fire, she took it out to show to Grae again.

"Probably I was holding it right the minute when the whale was coming here," she told him.

When a squeak came into the whale's breathing, she asked if that meant it was recovering.

"Could be, I guess," Grae said.

The squeak grew louder. She realized that Grae was listening to the blows intently. Several times when they went back from their breaks, he touched the whale's skin as if he was testing it.

"I think it's overheating," he burst out at last.

"Why didn't you say so before?"

"Because there's nothing we can do about it."

"We can get new bailers. These have got so floppy."

"New bailers won't make that much difference."

"We're walking too far. Walking eats the time up."

"What else are we going to do?"

"Stay in one place."

"Part of it won't get any water at all then."

"It will if we throw instead of carry."

"Won't it be hurt?"

"It shouldn't be. It's used to storms."

The throwing worked fine. They could get the water up and over the whale's back, in fact. They could make the water fly in sprays and showers.

With the whale's whole body visible, all Keri could think was how their task was heroic. She even said the word over to herself a couple of times.

She had to admit the steam from the whale's breathing wasn't going so high any more, and the blows seemed more of an effort. But she just worked faster, driving herself to bend and lift without pausing, inspiring herself with a picture of the girl in a force nine gale. She made the picture so the girl was nailing the roof back on her tilt with the wind howling and the sleet lashing all around her, desperate to make sure her baby was kept dry.

Keri and Grae were out towards the whale's tail by then. Its tail flukes were spread flat between them.

"Low tide's any minute. Just keep at it," she ordered.

Low tide came and went. The waterline on the whale's side was growing noticeably higher. When Grae went up to The Banks to pee, Keri held the bone for a moment as she made a prayer.

"We could do with some clouds, at least."

None appeared. She searched the sky above her hard, because the whale's breathing had a hesitation to it. Standing by its side, she could hear the air going into it. When the next break came, without saying anything to each other, she and Grae simply switched sides and worked on through.

Not once had Keri thought what they would do when it was time to go home. At five-thirty

Grae came to her, twisting his bailers in his hands.

"We should be leaving."

"If we go now, we might as well not have bothered."

"I know, but..."

"The whale needs us."

The sound of the next blow proved how right she was. Hanging his head, Grae waded into the water, but when they were switching later, Keri caught him standing, dawdling, biting his lip.

"When Mum comes to get us, we can explain maybe."

"Comes to get us? She never ever has."

"We've never not gone home."

"She'll be raging. 'Let them stew in their own juice,' she'll say."

"You don't think if we just went...just went and told her. Just...say, one of us."

"For God's sake stop fussing."

"There's the roast though."

"Can't you get it through your head the whale's more important?"

"It's not my stomach I'm thinking of."

"I don't care what you're thinking of. Stop wasting time."

To be certain he wouldn't change his mind, she watched him until he had filled his bailers.

All of a sudden it came to her then how tired she was. Her arms felt like lead. It hurt to lift them. To keep herself going, she had to start counting—two bailerfuls, four, six, eight to a hundred and back to two again. When that failed, she tried pretending that Gran was alive and she was telling her the story—"I bet we worked as hard as you did."

Still the sun shone. The air seemed to be growing hotter. The whale's breathing wasn't the only sign that it was having difficulty. Its eyelids had sunk down so its eyeballs were covered over. It wasn't watching any longer.

When a picture of the girl came to Keri, she seemed different. She was huddling into herself, doing her chores as if she could hardly get herself to move. The baby wasn't laughing. It was crying.

Six. Six-thirty. The sun might be hot, but the water was still cold. Keri saw that although Grae had put his sweatshirt and jacket back on, his teeth were chattering and his lips were turning blue.

She wasn't much better off herself. There

was only one thing for it. They had to get warm. With not taking breaks, they hadn't even been to the fire, so it had burned almost to nothing. The driftwood they could collect easily was finished.

Now's when we'll take what's nearest, Keri thought, as she gathered as many roof parts as she could.

By blowing on the embers, she got a blaze going quickly, but warming themselves seemed to take forever.

"We're going to have to start having breaks again," she said.

The next two blows the whale made came right on top of each other. Afterwards there was a long pause. Their eyes met while they held their own breaths waiting.

The sun was getting to where it was over the clifftops behind the wharf.

"I hope my rabbits are all right," Grae murmured. She had no answer. "I did give them extra, but..." His voice trailed off.

Seven. Seven-fifteen. The minutes between breaks were beginning to seem like hours. The muscles in Keri's shoulders were on fire. The next high tide wasn't till ten. Three hours away.

They needed more food. She'd started dividing the apples into halves to have between sandwich times. There was only one left now. They'd had to drink the first flask of hot chocolate when they'd been so cold. The sandwiches were dwindling.

The pieces from the roof were burning all too fast. Getting the lumber from the stage was easier said than done because so many of the boards were still nailed together, and the pieces were awkward to carry. She and Grae didn't want to leave the whale any longer than they had to, so they could only bring the wood in fits and starts. The effort left them more exhausted. When the board with her great-great-grandfather's initials appeared, she heaved it onto the pile with everything else.

Every so often Grae stopped to study the whale's skin again.

The sun was creeping towards the headland. Their jeans were almost dry. As Keri wrestled herself into them, she put her hand into her pocket.

She saw the girl inside the tilt. The baby wasn't even crying. It was whimpering—a sort of grizzle that sounded like it would never stop.

The girl was rocking it, but she had great dark circles under her eyes.

A quarter to eight. Eight. Eight-fifteen. At last the air was growing cooler. The sun hung in a golden ball, making a path of rippling brightness on the water. It blazed for a moment behind the headland and was gone. The shadows lengthened. A flock of gulls came quarrelling and calling to roost on The Raggeds.

A star gleamed in the west. Another appeared and another. The evening dampness oozed out of the stones, the rocks and the cliffs to seep into them. Keri and Grae came to the fire more often and they had to stay longer. The light was fading to greyness. Grae tripped and scraped his shins. He was stumbling all the time now.

When they got to the fire, she gave him another half sandwich and a whole cup of hot chocolate without caring whether it was time or not.

Night fell on them completely. Beyond the circle of the flames there was blackness.

"I'm worried," Grae muttered.

"Nothing's going to get you."

———

"It isn't the dark."

"Well, if it isn't the dark, what is it?"

Keri heard him swallow. "Mum."

"She can rage all she likes. She can't do anything. She's not here."

"That's the point. I don't know why she isn't. It's hours past when we ought to have been home for supper."

"I told you."

"I know what you told me, but I can't imagine her just...abandoning us. I've been waiting and waiting." He seemed so wretched that she put her arm around him.

Truth to tell, Keri had been wondering about Mum herself. More than once before the light went, she had caught herself glancing towards the headland expecting to see Mum, her hair all flying, tearing down the track.

"It's not that she's never been riled before," Grae went on.

The whale's blow broke in on them.

"We've got to get back to it," Keri said.

They went, but when they came to the fire next, Grae just sort of crumbled.

"High tide can't be long. It can't be," Keri blurted.

"I know," he answered, as she took up her bailers. "I'll come in a minute."

She would have nagged at him, but she could see it was no use. His face had gone grey. His arms were hanging limp, his hands were resting on his knees. He was younger. He needed more looking after. The minute stretched further.

"You've had long enough," she insisted.

"I know," he repeated.

Once more she set off by herself, but she couldn't get on the same without him. Soon she too was sitting in the warmth of the flame light.

"We'll go back to it at high tide. Maybe we've done enough. Maybe now it will only want launching," she said. Grae moved closer. "Can you see your watch?" she asked him.

He twisted his arm a bit. "I won't let us miss the tide, I promise."

Keri's hand went to her pocket. Her fingers closed around the bone and held it tightly. The girl was sitting beside the baby's bed, running her hand through the feathers. There was a blank, deep silence in the tilt.

Nine

"FIFTEEN minutes," Grae said.

With an effort, they managed to get themselves down to the water's edge as the waves reached the line of seaweed.

"At least it's not trying to push itself up farther," Keri noted, but she could tell from the shallow sound the blows made—as if the air was only going halfway into the whale's lungs—that it was no use trying to push it off. They waited until they could tell the tide had started to go down again.

"Maybe the next high tide, she suggested.

Her foot touched one of their dropped bailers. She thought about starting in once more with the water, but the darkness was too daunting. "If we can get through the night, we can do more in the morning. Maybe if we sleep a bit. Maybe we'll do better for some real resting."

"On the beach?"

"People lived here."

"They had houses. Shelters."

Once more she led him to the fire. They hunched against each other and dozed off. Again Keri dreamed. In the dream there was shouting.

When Grae shifted and leaned against her, she woke to find that the shouts were real. There was a light too, moving down the track towards them. The shouts came from whoever was carrying it. Thoughts of Duffys filled her mind.

She prodded Grae to rouse him so they could get ready. The whale would need defending. He stirred and woke slowly. The shouts had been going on for ages before she realized they held words.

"Grae. Grae, Keri!"

"Mum," Grae called. He would have gone to meet their mother, but she was coming too quickly.

"What the devil do you think you're up to?" she demanded.

Her voice was so angry that Keri was on her feet in an instant. "Doing something important." All her weariness was gone.

"Important? I'll give you important."

"There's a whale. We're rescuing it."

"Looks more like camping out to me."

"We worked all day."

"You didn't answer when I called you."

"We were sleeping."

"Sleeping?" Mum's voice shook. "I thought you'd fallen off the rocks and drowned."

A new sound rose from the whale—a moan that hung in the air and faded.

"What the hell's that?" Mum burst out. She sent the beam of the flashlight searching.

"What do you think it is? It's the whale. I told you."

"What have you been doing to it?"

Before Keri could answer, there was a second moan.

"Something's hurting it," she shouted, starting to run.

Mum and Grae came close behind her.

"There, see? That's where it is," Grae said.

As the glare of the flashlight beam lit up the whale's body, Keri closed her eyes.

"It wasn't like this before!"

Her eyes opened. The flashlight moved on farther.

There were cracks all over the whale's skin. A great welt ran from the fin on its back, glinting and shining where the flesh was open. Its body lay heaped and formless.

"The bones are breaking," Grae cried out.

"It hasn't moved. How can they be?" Keri demanded.

"It can't support itself on land. It needs the water. Its weight's too heavy. It can't hold itself up any more. It's collapsing."

Mum held the flashlight on the whale a moment longer.

"You can't save that," she said.

"If we'd gone on keeping it wet," Keri insisted.

"I don't think so," Grae put in.

"We just have to start up again..."

She grabbed him by the sleeve. When he tried to pull his arm out of her grasp, she kept on tugging.

"Ker," he said, "Ker, it isn't any use." Still she wouldn't let go. He had to wrench himself away from her. "I can't look at it any more." The words broke sobbing from him as he headed up the beach. Mum hesitated, then went after him.

Before Keri had even put her hand in her pocket, she got a picture of the girl, her child in her arms. She was standing in the doorway. The baby's body wasn't moving.

"Mum," Keri whispered.

The girl opened her mouth. A sound came from her. It filled the cove with high, thin wailing.

"Mum," Keri called louder, but her mother didn't hear.

The girl walked up towards the hillside. She bent and laid the body of her baby on the earth. The sound grew louder.

Keri went running. "MUM!"

When her mother stopped and turned, Keri flung herself forward. She rested her forehead against the bony hard place high up between her mother's breasts. She breathed in the cold, damp smell of Mum's jacket. Mum clasped her more tightly.

"Some mother I am," she muttered. "Feeling so self-righteous. Eating my supper even I was so riled. Letting it get dark. And you could have drowned." The words kept coming. Mum had brought blankets for them. "I almost set out empty-handed, you know that?" She gave them soup. "It's not just tonight either, is it? I've made your lives a misery. Sure, you've been difficult, but I'm the adult."

All Keri could think was how once long ago in a thunderstorm, when Grae was frightened, Mum had made up a song for them. How there was no other mother with a song like that.

You're two of the wonderful wonderfuls
You're two of the wonderful kids
You're two of the wonderful wonderfuls
You're two of the saucepan lids.

"Mum," she blurted. "Mum, sing Saucepan Lids."

Tears came to Mum's eyes. They glinted so Keri could see them in the firelight.

"I'd thought you'd have forgotten," she exclaimed.

"How could I forget? It's the stupidest song ever."

Mum's legs seemed to go out from under her. She sat on the beach and wept. At first Keri was too frightened to move. Then she went and put her arms around her mother's shoulders. She felt the boniness there as well. Mum's weeping carried on, and then it was over.

"We've got a home to get to," she said, blowing her nose. "You finish up that soup, the pair of you. Have a warm for the journey and we'll get started. It'll take us long enough, the state you've got yourselves into."

There had been no more moans coming from down by the water, but there had been the noises of breathing.

"What about the whale?" Keri asked.

"Isn't it enough you've half killed your-selves?" Mum demanded.

At first, she looked as if she was going to go on stuffing the backpack, but she put it down to come and give Keri a fierce, quick hug.

"There isn't anything you can do for it, my girl. You know that, don't you?" Through her own tears, Keri nodded. "We should at least go and see it."

Mum glanced at Grae. "We should really. I'm all right now," he said.

Spreading the embers, Mum gave in. When they got near the water's edge she held the flashlight so they could look at the whale again. Its body was more sunken, the cracks more evi-dent. The welt had crept down farther.

"There wasn't anything we could do for it ever, most like," Grae declared.

Still, they lingered. The next breath had a push-ing grunt to it. Suddenly Keri saw Gran in the hospital, lying pale as the bed sheets, not talking, not even responding when Keri took her hand.

"If it's going to die, why doesn't it just get on with it?" she burst out.

"Everything's got to take its time, I guess." Mum sighed.

There was a pause and the rattle of Grae's boots, shuffling on the beach stones.

"We won't be able to bury it, will we?"

"We have to call Fisheries. They'll tow it away. It'd be here forever otherwise, rotting and stinking."

The whale seemed to fall in on itself still further. Grae stepped forward to touch it, changed his mind and drew back.

"I wish there was something for goodbye," he murmured, as they turned and started up the track.

Mum had been right. The journey did seem to take forever. Keri's body ached all over. She thought she would never make it even though they took so many pauses for catching their breaths, but at last they were at the top and stopping for one more look.

Mum's gaze went out across the water. "Your dad's out there," she said.

"I wish he wasn't," Keri insisted.

"Me too," Mum replied. "But the men have always gone from here, you know that? Your grandad went for the sealing off the Labrador.

There's some went to America. Not only the men either. There's coming and going always."

Keri's thoughts went to the wharf. To how there was nothing on it and nothing to build anything with either. She could hear the whale still faintly, moaning again—its moans its breath now. She let her hand go to her pocket. The girl was on the clifftop, lying on the grass and resting. She was all by herself, but her face was turned to catch the sun.

Keri squeezed the bone harder. As always, the sharp points at the broad end dug into her palm. Tilting her head back, looking upwards, she saw that the sky was filled with stars.

As they crossed the headland, she let go of the bone and slipped her hand into her mother's. The turnaround in the road came. Maybe, Keri thought, Mum'll let us have the day off tomorrow. Maybe she'll phone in sick herself.

Below them, Prouty lay in darkness. In Gran's old house, at Alice's, even Duffys', everyone slept. There was just one house that was shining through every window. Keri held her mother's hand more tightly.

"You kept the lights on, Mum," she said.

———

ACKNOWLEDGEMENTS

Keri has taken many years to write. It would perhaps not have been possible without the financial assistance provided by the Canada Council, the Ontario Arts Council and the Regional Municipality of Ottawa-Carleton.

I thank Dr. Peter Beamish of Ocean Contact Limited, Trinity Bay, for his information about whales, and Lloyd and Annette Miller of Riverside Lodge, Trouty, for the time spent talking about daily life. Special thanks go to Lloyd for taking me out in his boat on cold grey mornings and sharing his knowledge of the sea. I also thank Eric West of North By East Productions for reading the manuscript and giving advice about the language of Newfoundland. I have not tried to reproduce this language but merely to give some sense of its strength.

My publishers have shown patience beyond belief. Always, their concern has been that the book should have the time to be the best that it might be. Its development owes much to Shelley Tanaka's tact and wisdom as editor. She has known how to suggest exactly those deletions and additions that would help me see my way.

The members of my writing group—Karleen Bradford, Rachna Gilmore and Caroline Parry—have been generous, supportive and above all wonderfully critical. Not once did they demand to know how I could possibly be rewriting each chapter yet again.

When a book takes years, it is not always easy for a writer to believe that the work will ever successfully be accomplished. When I lost my faith, I could always turn to my partner, Jennifer Cayley. She looked to the spirit rather than the failing paragraph and gave me courage to go on.

There is another person who must be named and that is my mother, Ina Ellins. She is the one who created "Saucepan Lids." She is a lover of life and laughter, and I pay her tribute now.